This book was made especially for:

❖ Theodore ❖

Dear Theodore,

How curious and brave you are! A wonderful journey awaits you in the pages of this book. Travel among some of the world's most fascinating countries and take it all in—but be sure to return home at the end! It would never be the same here without you.

With love:

Brave and intrepid,
Theodore set out
to explore the world
piece by piece.
What marvelous wonders
were in his first stop:
the land of the ancients
called Greece!

 **CAN YOU FIND
THEODORE
IN GREECE?**

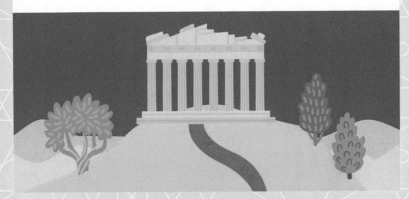

THESSALONIKI

Nestos

Haliacmon

Pineios

LARISSA

PATRAS

ATHENS

KALAMATA

OIA

RHODES

GREECE

HERAKLION

N
W E
S

To Iceland next he rowed and rowed, 'til Theodore saw volcanoes and ice. He would have stayed there the whole year long—the hot springs were so warm and nice!

 CAN YOU FIND THEODORE IN ICELAND?

ICELAND

ÍSAFJÖRÐUR

SAUÐÁRKRÓKUR

AKUREYRI

EGILSSTAÐIR

BORGARNES

REYKJAVÍK

KEFLAVÍK

SELFOSS

But on he sailed to Germany next, an old-fashioned, storybook treat. There was gingerbread, bratwurst, streudel, and schnitzel— so many *great* things to eat!

CAN YOU FIND THEODORE IN GERMANY?

GERMANY

ROSTOCK

HAMBURG

Elbe

BREMEN

Ems

HANNOVER

Berlin

Oder

Spree

ESSEN

LEIPZIG

KÖLN

DREZDEN

Weser

FRANKFURT AM MAIN

Rhine

STUTTGART

Danube

MÜNCHEN

N W E S

To Brazil he went next
just in time to explore
the magic of Carnival!
What lights, what
costumes, what music
there was!
But with the tide, he
soon left it all.

 CAN YOU FIND THEODORE IN BRAZIL?

Across the world to Japan the ship went, an island of tradition and tech.
He climbed up Mt. Fuji, tried sushi and fish, then took flight for the rest of his trek!

CAN YOU FIND THEODORE IN JAPAN?

JAPAN

日本

SAPPORO

AOMORI

AKITA

SENDAI

NIIGATA

TOKYO

YOKOHAMA

NAGOYA

OSAKA

HIROSHIMA

KOCHI

FUKUOKA

NAGASAKI

MIYAZAKI

YAKUSHIMA

OKINAWA

ISHIGAKI

Off to the Netherlands he flew on his kite to see the tulips and dikes. He fished and tried waffles and watched the windmills, then sped off on his new Dutch bike!

CAN YOU FIND THEODORE IN THE NETHERLANDS?

Netherlands

The next stop was Spain, and can you even believe it? The bulls ran the streets in Pamplona.
He gazed at the paintings and artistic feats in Madrid, Bilbao, and Barcelona.

 CAN YOU FIND THEODORE IN SPAIN?

To the green isle of Ireland Theodore went next.
The castles were something to see!
He kissed an old stone and joined in a jig, then set sail once again on the sea.

 CAN YOU FIND THEODORE IN IRELAND?

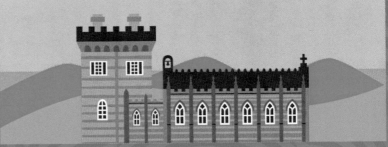

GALWAY

DUBLIN

Shannon

Barrow

KILKENNY

LIMERICK

WATERFORD

Suir

CORK

IRELAND

In Italy he landed
and to his surprise,
the country was
shaped like a boot!
In Rome, he did as
the Romans do,
and ate pasta,
gelato, and . . . fruit.

 **CAN YOU FIND
THEODORE IN
ITALY?**

Italy

Hong Kong was next, and the buildings there shone with business and commerce and light. Theodore had dumplings and criss-crossed the ferry, then set sail again in the night.

 CAN YOU FIND THEODORE IN HONG KONG?

HONG KONG

齒留香

單眼佬涼茶

KOWLOON

TSIM
SHA
TSUI

CENTRAL

MID-LEVEL

VAN CHAI

I ♥ 香港

VICTORIA PEAK

HAPPY VALLEY

The ship arrived in Denmark at last, a place nearly surrounded by sea! He saw the Tin Soldier and brave Little Mermaid and had tea with the prince and the queen.

 CAN YOU FIND THEODORE IN DENMARK?

SKAGEN

AALBORG

DENMARK

RANDERS

Storå

Gudenå

AARHUS

HERNING

HORSENS

Varde

VEJLE

ESBJERG

KOLDING

ODENSE

SVENDBORG

COPENHAGEN

ROSKILDE

RØNNE

N

W   E

S

T hen on, on to France, where the lavender grew and the tower called Eiffel stood tall. From Paris to Nice, Theodore saw every inch—he wanted to take in it all!

 CAN YOU FIND THEODORE IN FRANCE?

FRANCE

LILLE

RENNES

NANTES

PARIS

STRASBOURG

BORDEAUX

LYON

MONTPELLIER

TOULOUSE

MARSEILLE

NICE

Across the Atlantic his little craft went to the shores of old Mexico.
He danced to the sounds of the mariachi band (with his ears tucked inside his sombrero).

CAN YOU FIND THEODORE IN MEXICO?

Back in his balloon, he sailed through the night until reaching the land of his own. He snuggled in bed and dreamed all night long of the wonderful earth he called home!

 IF YOU COULD TRAVEL ANYWHERE, WHERE WOULD *YOU* WANT TO VISIT?

GERMANY

BRAZIL

ITALY

DENMARK

JAPAN 日本

GREECE

ICELAND

MEXICO

FRANCE

LONDON

Cover and book design by David Miles

Artwork created using elements from the following talented Shutterstock.com artists: Italy, Ireland, Spain, Netherlands, Greece, Iceland, Denmark, and Germany maps (Beskova Ekaterina); rabbit face (Sko Helen); hot air balloon (Iyeyee); around the world (R-i-s-e); falling stars (Nina_FOX); Mexico poster (Doni Hariyanto); Italy poster, France poster, Amsterdam poster, Germany poster (alaver); Denmark poster (Stanislav Novoselov); Hong Kong poster (Vector Tradition); Ireland poster (nastyrekh); Spain poster (Pavel Smolyakov); Japan poster (Ikanimo); Brazil poster (Anthony Krikoryan); Iceland poster (Red monkey); Greece poster (Anita_MI); bed, orange tree, houseplants, dresser, lamp (Ardea-studio); French pattern (traffico); Mexico elements (Katflare); Mexican pattern (Moon Meadows); Mexcio typography (Julio Aldana); Mexico map (helgascandinavus); Paris buildings, Golden Gate Bridge (Olga Zakharova); France map (lesyaskripak); Denmark pattern (PACPUMI); Hong Kong pattern (LauraKick); bamboo (VikiVector); Italian pattern (image4stock); fishing boat (Little Monster 2070); Irish pattern (Volodymyr Leus); Spanish pattern (Iva Villi); bunny on bicycle (svinka); Netherlands pattern (Ms Moloko); Japan pattern (marukopum); Japanese kites (Elsbet); cherry trees (Daiquiri); Japanese wave pattern (NokHoOkNoi); Japan typography (geen graphy); Japan and Hong Kong maps (Wondermilkycolor); Brazil pattern (EastFire); German pattern (dinadankersdesign); Iceland pattern (Yurta); Greece pattern (ALYOHAE); red bus (Gareth Cowlin); Eiffel tower and Notre-Dame (Anastasiia Kucherenko); Taipei locations (JoyImage); Brazil map (GoodStudio); miscellaneous world landmarks (Rimma Z).